Dear Parent:
Your child's love of reading starts here!

Every child learns to read in a different way and at his or her own speed. Some go back and forth between reading levels and read favorite books again and again. Others read through each level in order. You can help your young reader improve and become more confident by encouraging his or her own interests and abilities. From books your child reads with you to the first books he or she reads alone, there are I Can Read Books for every stage of reading:

SHARED READING
Basic language, word repetition, and whimsical illustrations, ideal for sharing with your emergent reader

BEGINNING READING
Short sentences, familiar words, and simple concepts for children eager to read on their own

READING WITH HELP
Engaging stories, longer sentences, and language play for developing readers

READING ALONE
Complex plots, challenging vocabulary, and high-interest topics for the independent reader

ADVANCED READING
Short paragraphs, chapters, and exciting themes for the perfect bridge to chapter books

I Can Read Books have introduced children to the joy of reading since 1957. Featuring award-winning authors and illustrators and a fabulous cast of beloved characters, I Can Read Books set the standard for beginning readers.

A lifetime of discovery begins with the magical words "I Can Read!"

Visit www.icanread.com for information
on enriching your child's reading experience.

For Erica and Laura—
city mouse, country mouse!
—A.S.C.

HarperCollins®, ☞®, and I Can Read Book® are trademarks of HarperCollins Publishers Inc.

Library of Congress Cataloging-in-Publication Data
Capucilli, Alyssa Satin
  Biscuit visits the big city / story by Alyssa Satin Capucilli ; pictures by Pat Schories.— 1st ed.
     p.   cm.— (My first I can read)
  Summary: On his first visit to the city, an excited puppy sees tall buildings, hears loud buses, and tries to say hello to everyone he meets.
     ISBN-10: 0-06-074164-3 — ISBN-13: 978-0-06-074164-8
     ISBN-10: 0-06-074165-1 (lib. bdg.) — ISBN-13: 978-0-06-074165-5 (lib. bdg.)
     ISBN-10: 0-06-074166-X (pbk.) — ISBN-13: 978-0-06-074166-2 (pbk.)
     [1. Dogs—Fiction. 2. City and town life—Fiction.] I. Schories, Pat, ill. II. Title. III. Series: My first I can read book.
PZ7.C179Bist 2006   2005002662
[E]—dc22   CIP
                                                                                                    AC

❖

I Can Read!™

SHARED
My
First
READING

Biscuit
Visits
the
Big City

story by ALYSSA SATIN CAPUCILLI
pictures by PAT SCHORIES

HarperCollinsPublishers

6

Here we are, Biscuit.

Woof, woof!

We're in the big city.

We're going to visit
our friend Jack.

8

Woof, woof!

Coo, coo!

9

Stay with me, Biscuit.

It's very busy in the big city!

Woof, woof!

11

There are lots of tall buildings
in the big city, Biscuit.
Woof, woof!

There are lots of people, too.
Woof, woof!

Funny puppy!
You want to say hello
to everyone.

15

Stay with me, Biscuit.

It's very busy here!

Woof, woof!

Beep! Beep!

Woof!

It's only a big bus, Biscuit.

Woof, woof!
You found the fountain,
Biscuit.

There's so much to see
in the big city,
isn't there, Biscuit?

Woof!

Coo, coo!

Woof, woof!

Coo, coo!

21

Woof, woof! Woof, woof!

Oh no, Biscuit! Come back!

Biscuit, where are you going?

Woof!

Silly puppy! Here you are.

This is a big, busy city, Biscuit.
But you found our friend Jack,
and some new friends, too!

Coo, coo!

Woof!